BELLE

The Amazing, Astonishingly Magical Journey of an Artfully Painted Lady

MARY LEE CORLETT

illustrated by PHYLLIS SAROFF

BUNKER HILL PUBLISHING

DEDICATIONS

Mary Lee Corlett: *For Victoria*

Phyllis Saroff: *For my father*

ACKNOWLEDGMENTS

We would like to thank our families and the many friends and colleagues, especially those at the National Gallery of Art, whose support and enthusiasm made this book possible.

All works of art reproduced courtesy of the National Gallery of Art, Washington.

www.bunkerhillpublishing.com
First published in 2011
by Bunker Hill Publishing Inc.
285 River Road, Piermont
New Hampshire 03779, USA

10 9 8 7 6 5 4 3 2 1

Library of Congress Control Number: 2011925662

ISBN 10: 1-59373-084-5
ISBN 13: 978-1-59373-084-0

Published in the United States by Bunker Hill Publishing
Designed by Peter Holm, Sterling Hill Productions
Printed in China by Jade Productions

"Every artist wants his work to be permanent, but what is? Venice is sinking. Great books and pictures were lost in the Florence floods. In the meantime, we still enjoy the butterflies."

ROMARE BEARDEN
American Artist (1911–1988)

Hovering can be very tricky! Especially when you've been
doing it in the same spot for more than three hundred years!
My name is Belle, and the truth be told, . . .

I have been *here* – in this art museum –
since about 1960.

But my world actually began long before that, in about 1660, in a place in Europe known as Flanders, when an artist named Jan Davidsz de Heem put me into this painting.

And so I have been in this still life picture ever since, eager to land on that big, feathery white poppy, so close I can *almost* taste it, but I can never reach it. Very frustrating! Still, in three hundred years I have been a very good butterfly and stayed exactly where I was put. I never strayed. Except once.

One of the most wonderful things about being a butterfly, a real butterfly anyway, has to be *metamorphosis* – the magical change that happens between creeping along on caterpillar legs and soaring high on butterfly wings. But because I am a *painted* lady, I never made that change. I have always been a butterfly, always had wings, although in 300 years I'd never actually *fluttered* them. That is, until that *one* day.

Because of what happened on that *one* day, I realized for the first time that I, too, could change. I didn't even have to be a butterfly. Because I am a *painted* lady, I can be anything. On that one exciting day I transformed myself more times than I can count and had the best adventure of my life!

It was early in the morning – the art museum hadn't even opened yet – and the museum staff (the art handlers) had taken our painting down from its usual place on the wall to go to the Conservation Studio, where they clean you up, check you out, and repair you if you need it. For a painting the Conservation Studio is part hospital, part spa. Maybe something about our painting was unstable. (Maybe we were scheduled for an x-ray?)

We rolled across the gallery on that cart, heading for the elevators. I felt a sudden jolt, a strange little jostle, a mysterious *whoosh* of air, and the next thing I knew I was flying!

I cannonballed through the air in a tight little blob; then it occurred to me to stretch my wings, and suddenly I was flying free! I'm sure I'd have kept going, too, except for the "Ouch!" behind me. When I heard that cry, I circled back.

Apparently, I wasn't the only butterfly to be bumped.

"I was just hanging out," Brimstone complained, "Minding my own business as I always have, when BAM, suddenly I was tossed off the tulip! I didn't even have time to right myself before I hit the floor.

"Ouch!" he said again for emphasis, as he rubbed his bruised wing.

"What about Salamander, Snail, or Bee? Did they pop off, too?" I asked.

"I don't know, but the ants held their ground. The spider swayed a bit on the end of his web, but I think he stayed on. So did the caterpillar. I saw that much before our painting rolled away."

"Poor Spider," I giggled, "After 300 years of dangling like a snack on a string in front of that hungry-looking Salamander I'll bet he wishes *he*'d popped off too!"

But then I stopped laughing, because that's when Brimstone's words – "the painting rolled away" – finally registered in my brain. "Hey! Where did our painting go?!" I cried. I frantically looked around and spied it at the end of a long hall. "Follow that cart!"

"Hold the elevator!" Brimstone shouted as he pointed, but he never even had time to get up off the floor. It was already too late. The elevator doors closed and our painting was GONE.

"Uh-Oh." I tried to remain calm, but Brimstone didn't. "What do we do NOW?" he wailed. "We have to get back to our places. The composition won't be complete without us!"

"I guess we'll just have to find the Conservation Studio ourselves," I said with more confidence than I felt. After all, at this point I hadn't even logged a full minute of flight time, and yet if you compared my aviation skills to Brimstone's, I was an expert.

"But which way do we go?" I wondered. I'd certainly been carted through the museum on other occasions, but for me the building had always been a confusing maze of long corridors, twisting passageways, large rooms, and small niches. But because one of the art handlers always drove the cart, I never had any reason to pay attention to routes.

"Do you suppose there's anyone else in this gallery who knows the way?" Brimstone asked. I looked around, trying to think, but all the whistling and chirping coming from the open case above us was making that difficult. Brimstone noticed it, too. "There must be a full orchestra of birds up there," he said. "In a crowd that big, surely *someone* will know the way. I'll just go inquire."

Then, before I could remind him that in some circles "butterfly" was just another name for "bird food," he launched into his first flight. It was a wobbly takeoff, but somehow he managed to gain altitude, and he headed straight for the *Concert of Birds*.

He careened into the painting, hitting it hard and at a weird angle. He hit it so hard, in fact, that he bounced right off the surface.

Brimstone didn't even leave a smudge, but he must have given the art a bit of a jolt. I was discovering how dangerous this jostling was for paintings with apparently delicate constitutions.

Brimstone hit the gallery floor for the second time that morning – while the bump to the painting caused this bird to pop off!

The bird shot into the air and didn't see Brimstone drop to the floor, but unfortunately for me I was still airborne. That bird caught sight of me instantly. "Well, well," he crowed. "You're just in time for breakfast. Mine!" And he set a course straight for me. I knew I had to find some place to hide, and fast! I looked around to see where I might be able to blend in.

Brimstone still flitted around unsteadily on the floor, but he was wildly gesturing toward a painting on the wall.

"Look at that Lady!" he called out. "She's stopped writing and I think she's looking right at you! Maybe she will let you hide out with her!"

"Not my best colors," I shouted as I zoomed by. "But she's definitely got lots of yours. And . . . I think you'd better get up there fast. Now *you've* been spotted, too!" Brimstone looked up, his eyes widened to the size of saucers. That bird had changed course and was now heading straight for *him.*

Brimstone zigged, then zagged, but this time he was careful to land gently. And then something amazing happened.

Because he was paint and she was paint, Brimstone discovered he didn't have to sit on top and *hope* he would be camouflaged. "Hey! Look at me! I blend right in!" He was right! He *really* blended in. He actually changed himself, rearranged himself. He *became* one of her hair ribbons.

"Wow!" I thought. "I *definitely* have to try that!"

With Brimstone out of the picture – or actually, he was now in the picture – that bird had once again set his sights on me. I looked around frantically.

The *Girl with the Red Hat* was looking right at me. The lively sparkle in her eyes told me she would be willing to let me join her.

"Great hat!" I told her as I easily lost myself in the softness of the brim.

A little while later I heard Brimstone's hoarse whisper: "Pssssstttt! Do you think it's safe to come out yet?"

"How should I know?" I snapped. I was feeling waspish because I blamed him for releasing that bird. I emerged from the hat a little and didn't see the creature anywhere around, so I cautiously crept to the surface. "Let's go! Hurry!" I commanded, "before he comes back!"

And we were off once more, in search of the Conservation Studio and our own painting. We still didn't know how to get there; we were just winging it.

We flew into the next gallery and I thought about asking the boy leaning over the ledge, but he was concentrating so hard on what he was doing, I was afraid if we disturbed him we might pop his bubble. I sure didn't want to be responsible for that!

"Maybe the girl next door will help us," Brimstone said, pointing to the dignified young lady in a neighboring picture.

But then we BOTH noticed her DOG.

"He's sitting quietly and he looks well-behaved," Brimstone hedged. "So then, why do I feel so nervous? My stomach is fluttery!"

"Interesting," I thought. "A butterfly with 'butterflies.'"

"Maybe he won't see us?" I offered. "Maybe he *can't* see us with all that hair over his eyes." In the end we decided there was no point in begging the question by flying any closer. Sometimes you have to listen to your gut.

Just then I noticed two elegant women:

"Those gowns are splendid!" I complimented them. "Look at those sumptuous fabrics. It's hard to say which I like best." I was about to ask who made them, or if they had ever had to have restoration work, when Brimstone interrupted with a very rude, ear-piercing yell.

"DUCK!"

"That's no DUCK! That's THE BIRD!"

That winged demon had spotted me and was now bearing down at full speed. I didn't have much time. I would have to make a choice – NOW. So, even though both of the ladies' dresses were dazzling, I chose the striped gown, thinking as I melted into it that it was just *perfect* for me. Brimstone preferred the hat. Yes, very stylish, I thought.

The bird circled the gallery again and again but couldn't find us. He finally gave up and flew off. We waited. And waited. Afraid to breathe. At last Brimstone and I cautiously reemerged.

"We've got to get back to our painting," Brimstone declared in a hushed voice. "It's dangerous out here!"

We peered around the corner and spotted a studious-looking gentleman.

"Excuse me?" Brimstone asked in a strained whisper. "Did you happen to see a bird fly through here?"

But apparently the young man's lips were sealed.

"He's obviously not a talker, but I wonder if he'd let me borrow his glasses. He's got two pair after all. Do you suppose I would see better with them on?"

"Worth a try. Maybe then you could see across the hall to be sure the coast is clear."

"Love the geranium." I heard Brimstone say as he climbed in.

He morphed into the painting behind the glasses, but soon emerged shaking his head. "No luck. Everything is even more of a blur with those things. I can't even focus on my wing in front of my face."

With that bird in hot pursuit we decided it wasn't safe to linger.

When we flew into the next gallery, Brimstone exclaimed: "Hey! Not a single one of these paintings is hanging!"

He was right. "What's going on in here?" Brimstone wondered. "Why are these on the floor instead of the walls?"

"We've seen this sort of thing before," I reminded him. "I think the museum people are getting ready to hang them as an exhibition."

"Oh . . . Right!" Brimstone looked around. "Well, don't look now, but we are surrounded by men with no feet."

"Of course these men had feet! The artists just didn't paint them!"

"I know that! I was making a little joke! But," he observed, "do you think it's strange how many of them have one hand tucked into their coat? Do you think we've stumbled onto some sort of secret code?"

"Hmmm. . . ."

It does seem a little odd." I said. "Do you think they're giving us directions? Maybe they're trying to tell us where to find the Conservation Studio – most of them seem to be pointing to the right."

"It's hard to tell if they're pointing when you can't see their fingers." Brimstone was silent a moment. "You know, maybe it's not a sign. Maybe they don't have any pants pockets to put their hands in."

"Hmmm. . . ."

I pondered this, staring hard at them all for another full minute. "I think we should keep going. . . .

"To the right!"

"Okay."

"I think we're lost." Brimstone declared after a while.

"Nonsense." I insisted. "We'll be back in our painting soon." But to be safe, we found a painting we liked in each room, just in case the bird reappeared and we had to make another speedy transformation. We were discovering how much fun it was to be made of daubs of paint – a few touches of color, yet we could be so many things!

We could sink into these comfy chairs (not the one with the dog!)

Or I could be a hair ribbon.
Brimstone would be cute as a button.

Being a flower would be nice,

. . . especially in this colorful garden,

. . . or maybe a wagon or a flower pot!

"Hey, look at this one! Are they playing a game?" Brimstone wanted to know.

"I think it's *Hide and Seek.*"

"Looks like a *lot* of fun," I said.

"We have time to join them for a quick round, don't you think?" he suggested.

It turned out to be a good thing we did, too, because we had just entered into the game when that raptor returned, gliding silently into the gallery, slowly surveying the room, looking for *us*. Luckily, I had already concealed myself in the pattern of that luxurious rug, and Brimstone had morphed into the highlights on that lustrous glass lamp shade.

The bird drifted by the painting, so close I could see the glint in both of his hungry eyes. I almost shuddered in fear, but I was too afraid to move. He circled back.

"Oh no!" I thought, "Did he see us?" I held my breath, hoping we had truly managed to melt completely into our surroundings. *Finally*, he flew on. Whew! Our hiding places had done the trick!

We waited and watched to be sure the bird was really gone. Then we quietly emerged with renewed determination to find that Conservation Studio.

We rocketed into the next gallery, where we found a little girl.

She was so involved in her cooking that she took no interest in us, and I thought we shouldn't stir up trouble.

Yet Brimstone insisted on stopping to find out what was in her bowl. He landed for just a minute so he could have a quick look, but was disappointed when he couldn't figure it out. There was no more time to waste. He knew we had to move on, but he came away a little blue.

We journeyed on, but very soon *I* was the one who *had* to stop again. The bird didn't seem to be anywhere around – I hoped – and I couldn't bear to pass up *this* splashy landscape!

"Too much color for me." Brimstone said. "I'll just wait out here." And he hovered while I shimmied my way into the trees.

While I was bursting with glorious color I heard Brimstone talking to himself: "I wonder what it would be like to play in snow?"

I couldn't believe he went in there! Luckily the dogs weren't looking when he landed. But he sure didn't stay for long. He burst out on a gust of icy wind.

"Fffrreezing . . . in . . . thththere!" he shivered.

He flew away so fast I had to race to catch up to him in the next gallery.

But suddenly the bird rounded the corner right behind us, so Brimstone and I had to quickly plunge into the nearest painting.

There was plenty of pattern for both of us. So much, in fact, that we actually lost track of each other for a while. Finally, I popped off the tablecloth just in time to see Brimstone dive back into the wallpaper.

The whole time we were popping in and out we didn't see the bird, and we hoped he'd lost sight of us. But we were wrong! He knew exactly where we were – and he was plotting. That crazy bird was getting sneaky. He was lurking in the next gallery, waiting for us to come around the corner.

"Yikes!"

In the nick of time I managed to push myself deep into the biggest *Jack-in-the-Pulpit* you have ever seen. Yummy!

There were lots of possibilities for Brimstone in the painting he chose, but he didn't really like any of them.

So he was a little steamed at first.

Then he got frosty . . .

hung out on the fringes . . .

and tried on an apron and a shirt before he gave up and turned into a little baby.

Again we'd had a narrow escape, but as soon as we reemerged and tried to slip away, the bird was back on our trail. We were in big trouble because the bird had finally figured out that we always came out of the same painting we went into.

Now, every time we popped out, he was right there, waiting. He wasn't going to be fooled anymore. Just when I thought there was no hope, that we were truly doomed, that harebrained bird tried a new trick – for him, anyway – and luckily for us, it turned out to be his undoing.

This is what he did . . .

He decided to follow me into a painting. But at that moment I realized I was heading straight for another painting of birds and I panicked. I certainly didn't want to repeat Brimstone's earlier mistake, bump *another* painting wrong and release *more* avian trouble. So, at the last minute I dipped and dodged away. But the bird couldn't stop or change course. He flew right into that painting.

What happened next proves that birds don't know a thing about metamorphosing. Maybe because this particular painting *featured* birds, that bird's brain told him it would be okay.

The bird morphed in all right – but he never came back out. The painting kept him! This work of art captured the spirit of that bird perfectly!

"Do you think he'll ever come back?" Brimstone wondered, after much time had passed. We breathed a sigh of relief when we realized our pursuer had definitely been detained.

With the chase finally over, I was busy charting our next course when I discovered Brimstone had disappeared. I flitted around frantically. "Brimstone!" I called out in a panic.

"Here I am," he announced as he emerged out of a *Lavender Mist.* "You wouldn't believe all the delicate, interwoven layers of paint in there. It's like entering another world!"

"It does draw you in, that's for sure. And I'd love to stay, but we really have no more time to waste. We need to find our own painting, and soon!"

"Okay. But can we stop here first? I'd love to be the icing on *that* cake!" he said, pointing to the one with the ring of what looked like raspberries on top.

"Brimstone! You're *drooling?*" How undignified. "Come on! We don't have time for dessert!"

We were sure we were getting close to the Conservation Studio when we noticed a couple of characters. How could we miss them? Their painting was more than twice the size of ours and they were big and bold and – so comical. "I don't think we should count on them for accurate directions," Brimstone cautioned. "I wouldn't want to end up the butt of a joke!"

"You're probably right." I agreed.

"Look at that sculpture!" Brimstone said, as he flexed a wing and stretched out his own proboscis, then coiled it up again. "Do you think it's trying to tell us something?"

With my eyes I followed the contour of that elegant curl, which seemed to be pointing down the hallway. "There's our painting!" I cried. "It's going down the hall. Follow that cart!"

It was heading toward another bank of elevators. But this time we reached the cart *before* the elevator doors closed.

When the doors opened again on the next level, Brimstone and I were once again in our painting, exactly as we had been for three centuries. At last we were back where we belonged.

Can you believe it? We were never missed!

"Wow!" I said. "I've been a hat, a gown, a rug, a tree, a tablecloth, a flower, and of course, a lady butterfly."

"Not bad for a morning's work," Brimstone agreed.

After a moment, Brimstone quietly asked, "Belle?'"

"Yes, Brimstone?"

"Can we do this again?"

Sometimes he amazes me.

"Maybe so, Brimstone. But, how about if we wait another 300 years."

BELLE'S

Amazing, Astonishingly Magical Journ~~ey~~al

Dear Diary,

I have just returned home after an AMAZING journey, and I've got lots of pictures! But first, since diaries usually hold secrets, I am going to tell you a little secret about myself: I am not **really** a **Painted Lady**. Whoa! Are you surprised? Oh, to be sure I am an "artfully painted lady," that is, made of paint — but alas, I am NOT a "Painted Lady" butterfly. I'll show you. I am going to paste in a picture of a real **Painted Lady**:

(Not me!)

In strict "butterfly" terms then, I am a Red Admiral, like the butterfly in this picture:

Still, I find it a little odd to think of myself as an ADMIRAL — so I will just continue to think of myself as BELLE.

(Me!)

There really is a butterfly called **Brimstone**, though — just like my friend.

Now, with that little secret revealed, I am going to paste in all of the pictures I have from my magical journey — so I will always remember that amazing day at the National Gallery of Art!

Here we are at home — before our journey began! I know that people call this type of painting still life, but I think of it as a group portrait. Look! There I am! And there's Brimstone, and Salamander, and Spider, and The Ants! The painter obviously studied nature very closely to get our likenesses just right.

Vase of Flowers, c. 1660, Jan Davidsz de Heem (page 3)

Concert of Birds, 1660/1670, Circle of Jan van Kessel (page 9)

This is where we RAN INTO that Bird! Look! He's coming late to the Concert! How rude is THAT! It's hard to believe that such a HUGE avian MENACE could have been let loose from the teeny-tiny image in this painting. The whole picture is no bigger than a postcard!

So exciting! This was Brimstone's first metamorphosis! From WING to RIBBON — it was a picture-perfect change-up! And the Lady remained so serene during the entire episode!

A Lady Writing, c. 1665, Johannes Vermeer (page 11)

And this was MY first metamorphosis! Becoming part of the hat was fun! But it tickled! And here's another big secret, Diary — I wasn't alone in there! I haven't told anyone this until just now, but someone else was hiding in that painting with me!

Girl with the Red Hat, c. 1665/1666, Johannes Vermeer (page 12)

Here is an "x-ray" (the scientists call it an **infrared reflectogram**) taken in the Conservation Studio. You can see the image of the girl with the red hat, but down below her is my secret companion! Upside down! I like to look at this page upside down for the best view! My hidden friend likes big hats, too!

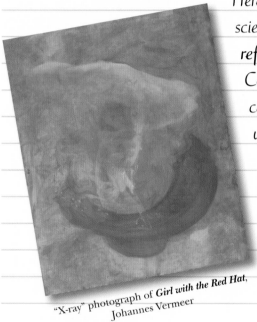

"X-ray" photograph of *Girl with the Red Hat*, Johannes Vermeer

Here we made sure to steer clear of that bubble! Too easy to accidentally pop — that bubble might have disappeared in one careless instant! Can you imagine this painting without it?? That would have been horrible, because there certainly wasn't "Pop Art" in the eighteenth century! (Hee! Hee!)

Soap Bubbles, probably 1733/1734, Jean Siméon Chardin (page 13)

María Teresa de Borbón y Vallabriga, later Condesa de Chinchón,
1783, Francisco de Goya (page 14)

I have to wonder if this little girl liked to wear all of those fancy clothes? They would make it hard to run and jump, and after all, she was only four years old! I'll bet her DOG was older than that! (Especially if you figure his age in "dog years.")

The Marquise de Pezay, and the Marquise de Rougé with Her Sons Alexis and Adrien,
1787, Elisabeth-Louise Vigée Le Brun (page 15)

Those dresses are so shimmery! The artist obviously had lots of practice painting luxurious fabrics and fashionable clothing. But then, she was the court painter for Queen Marie-Antoinette, so no wonder!

Brimstone discovered that he couldn't see a thing through those glasses Rubens holds! But neither could Rubens. His first pair corrected for **nearsightedness**, but he got the second pair when it turned out that he was actually **farsighted**! I think Rubens has both pairs of glasses in this painting because Rembrandt decided he wanted his brother to be wearing glasses instead of holding them — but he didn't want to risk ruining the composition by painting over the extra pair. I was thinking . . . those brothers' names seem familiar. . . . Oh, sure! There are paintings by Sir Peter Paul Rubens and Rembrandt van Rijn in the galleries. Same names but different artists!

Rubens Peale with a Geranium, 1801,
Rembrandt Peale (pages 16 and 17)

Captain Alexander Graydon, c. 1746,
Robert Feke (page 18)

John Lothrop, c. 1770,
John Durand (page 18)

John Harrisson, c. 1823,
Frederick W. Mayhew (page 19)

Obviously, the hand-in-the-coat was a popular pose!

Portrait of a Black Man, probably 1829 (page 19)

Hey! In this portrait you can look out a window and see the riverboat called "New Philadelphia"! That boat set speed records! And it was the first on the Hudson River to employ African Americans, like this distinguished gentleman!

I heard that this dog — a Belgian griffon — was the artist's pet. Why would anyone keep a dog around on purpose?! I wonder if it liked being an artist's model, or if it even stayed AWAKE long enough to know it was posing? At least it wasn't fidgety! ZZZZZZzzzzzzz……..

Little Girl in a Blue Armchair, 1878, Mary Cassatt (page 20)

A Girl with a Watering Can, 1876, Auguste Renoir (page 20)

This little girl is so charming, and radiant, and so well dressed! This painting is very popular with the museum visitors, so I was thrilled to have the chance to be a part of it for a little while!

I have always loved flowers — so it was amazing to discover Monet's garden. So full of light and the blooms! They were everywhere! Butterfly Paradise!

The Artist's Garden at Vétheuil, 1880, Claude Monet (page 21)

Hide and Seek, c. 1877,
James Jacques Joseph Tissot (page 22)

By the time we reached this painting, we'd
already had a fair amount of practice playing
Hide and Seek!

This one made Brimstone blue...I
think he was worried that she didn't
have enough food to eat...

Le Gourmet, 1901, Pablo Picasso (page 24)

But I had a fantastically wild time in this splashy landscape!

Mountains at Collioure, 1905, André Derain (page 25)

Siberian Dogs in the Snow, 1909/1910, Franz Marc (page 25)

It sure takes a lot of color to paint something WHITE! I think that's pretty cool! (Ha! Ha! Brimstone thought it was "cool," too!)

Brimstone and I chased each other in and out of these lively patterns so fast my head was spinning!

Pianist and Checker Players, 1924, Henri Matisse (page 26)

Jack-in-Pulpit - No. 2, 1930, Georgia O'Keeffe (page 27)

Can you believe the size of this flower! A butterfly's dream-come-true!

Interior, 1944, Horace Pippin (page 28)

Brimstone had a hard time deciding where he could best fit into this well-ordered room!

It was such a relief when that Bird finally found "new meaning" in this painting! Permanently! That is, at least as far as we know, he is still there. . . .

Hierarchical Birds, 1944, Mark Rothko (page 29)

"I was dripped, poured, and flung!"
Brimstone told me. He loved all that
ACTION.

Number 1, 1950 (Lavender Mist), 1950, Jackson Pollock (page 30)

Paint that looks THICK and
CREAMY and good enough
to eat! That is "icing on the
cake!" SWEET!

Cakes, 1963, Wayne Thiebaud (page 31)

No bubbles to pop here, but this style is called Pop Art because it takes its subject from "POPular culture!" The scene comes from a storybook called **Donald Duck Lost and Found**. I'll bet it's a really funny book!

Look Mickey, 1961, Roy Lichtenstein (page 31)

This sculpture speaks my language! And a good thing, too. It was better than GPS for guiding us home!

Lever No. 3, 1989, Martin Puryear (page 33)

Jan Davidsz de Heem, Dutch, 1606 – 1683/1684, ***Vase of Flowers***, c. 1660, oil on canvas, 69.6 × 56.5 cm (27⅜ × 22¼ in.), National Gallery of Art, Washington, Andrew W. Mellon Fund, 1961.6.1, (page 40)

Circle of Jan van Kessel, ***Concert of Birds***, 1660/1670, oil on copper, 13 × 18 cm (5⅛ × 7¹⁄₁₆ in.), National Gallery of Art, Washington, Gift of John Dimick, 1983.19.4, (page 40)

Johannes Vermeer, Dutch, 1632 – 1675, ***A Lady Writing***, c. 1665 oil on canvas, 45 × 39.9 cm (17¾ × 15¾ in.), National Gallery of Art, Washington, Gift of Harry Waldron Havemeyer and Horace Havemeyer, Jr., in memory of their father, Horace Havemeyer, 1962.10.1, (page 40)

Johannes Vermeer, Dutch, 1632 – 1675, ***Girl with the Red Hat***, c. 1665/1666, oil on panel, 22.8 × 18 cm (9 × 7¹⁄₁₆ in.), National Gallery of Art, Washington, Andrew W. Mellon Collection, 1937.1.53, (page 41)

Infrared reflectogram composite, Johannes Vermeer, Dutch, 1632 – 1675, ***Girl with the Red Hat***, 1937.1.53, Andrew W. Mellon Collection. Conservation Department, National Gallery of Art, Washington, (page 41)

Jean Siméon Chardin, French, 1699 – 1779, ***Soap Bubbles***, probably 1733/1734, oil on canvas, 93 × 74.6 cm (36⅝ × 29⅜ in.), National Gallery of Art, Washington, Gift of Mrs. John W. Simpson, 1942.5.1, (page 41)

Francisco de Goya, Spanish, 1746 – 1828, ***María Teresa de Borbón y Vallabriga, later Condesa de Chinchón***, 1783, oil on canvas, 134.5 × 117.5 cm (53 × 46¼ in.), National Gallery of Art, Washington, Ailsa Mellon Bruce Collection, 1970.17.123, (page 42)

Elisabeth-Louise Vigée Le Brun, French, 1755 – 1842, ***The Marquise de Pezay, and the Marquise de Rougé with Her Sons Alexis and Adrien***, 1787, oil on canvas, 123.4 × 155.9 cm (48⅝ × 61⅜ in.), National Gallery of Art, Washington,Gift of the Bay Foundation in memory of Josephine Bay Paul and Ambassador Charles Ulrick Bay, 1964.11.1, (page 42)

Rembrandt Peale, American, 1778 – 1860, ***Rubens Peale with a Geranium***, 1801, oil on canvas, 71.4 × 61 cm (28⅛ × 24 in.), National Gallery of Art, Washington, Patrons' Permanent Fund, 1985.59.1, (page 43)

Robert Feke, American, c. 1707 – c. 1751, ***Captain Alexander Graydon***, c. 1746, oil on canvas, 101.2 × 81 cm (40 x 32 in.), National Gallery of Art, Washington, Gift of Edgar William and Bernice Chrysler Garbisch, 1966.13.2, (page 43)

John Durand, American, active 1765/1782 ***John Lothrop***, c. 1770, oil on canvas, 90.8 × 70.6 cm (35¾ × 27¹³⁄₁₆ in.), National Gallery of Art, Washington, Gift of Edgar William and Bernice Chrysler Garbisch, 1980.62.70, (page 43)

Frederick W. Mayhew, American, 1785 – 1854, ***John Harrisson***, c. 1823, oil on canvas, 76 × 63.4 cm (29¹⁵⁄₁₆ × 24¹⁵⁄₁₆ in.), National Gallery of Art, Washington, Gift of Edgar William and Bernice Chrysler Garbisch, 1980.62.16, (page 43)

American, 19th Century, ***Portrait of a Black Man***, probably 1829, oil on wood, 49.5 × 34.3 cm (19½ × 13½ in.), National Gallery of Art, Washington, Gift of Edgar William and Bernice Chrysler Garbisch, 1953.5.22, (page 44)

Mary Cassatt, American, 1844 – 1926, ***Little Girl in a Blue Armchair***, 1878, oil on canvas, 89.5 × 129.8 cm (35½ × 51⅛ in.), National Gallery of Art, Washington, Collection of Mr. and Mrs. Paul Mellon, 1983.1.18, (page 44)

Auguste Renoir, French, 1841 – 1919, ***A Girl with a Watering Can***, 1876, oil on canvas, 100.3 × 73.2 cm (39½ × 28¾ in.), National Gallery of Art, Washington, Chester Dale Collection, 1963.10.206, (page 45)

Claude Monet, French, 1840 – 1926, ***The Artist's Garden at Vétheuil***, 1880, oil on canvas, 151.5 × 121 cm (59⅞ × 47⅝ in.), National Gallery of Art, Washington, Ailsa Mellon Bruce Collection, 1970.17.45, (page 45)

James Jacques Joseph Tissot, French, 1836 – 1902, ***Hide and Seek***, c. 1877, oil on wood, 73.4 × 53.9 cm (28⅞ × 21¼ in.), National Gallery of Art, Washington, Chester Dale Fund, 1978.47.1, (page 46)

Pablo Picasso, Spanish, 1881 – 1973, ***Le Gourmet***, 1901, oil on canvas, 92.8 × 68.3 cm (36½ × 26⅞ in.), National Gallery of Art, Washington, Chester Dale Collection, 1963.10.52, © 2011 Estate of Pablo Picasso / Artists Rights Society (ARS), New York, (page 46)

André Derain, French, 1880 – 1954, ***Mountains at Collioure***, 1905, oil on canvas, 81.3 × 100.3 cm (32 × 39½ in.), National Gallery of Art, Washington, John Hay Whitney Collection, 1982.76.4, © 2011 Artists Rights Society (ARS), New York / ADAGP, Paris, (page 47)

Franz Marc, German, 1880 – 1916, ***Siberian Dogs in the Snow***, 1909/1910, oil on canvas, 80.5 × 114 cm (31⅝ × 44⅞ in.), National Gallery of Art, Washington, Gift of Mr. and Mrs. Stephen M. Kellen, 1983.97.1, (page 47)

Henri Matisse, French, 1869 – 1954, ***Pianist and Checker Players***, 1924, oil on canvas, 73.7 × 92.4 cm (29 × 36⅜ in.), National Gallery of Art, Washington, Collection of Mr. and Mrs. Paul Mellon, 1985.64.25, © 2011 Succession H. Matisse / Artists Rights Society (ARS), New York (page 48)

Georgia O'Keeffe, American, 1887 – 1986, ***Jack-in-Pulpit - No. 2***, 1930, oil on canvas, 101.6 × 76.2 cm (40 × 30 in.), National Gallery of Art, Washington, Alfred Stieglitz Collection, Bequest of Georgia O'Keeffe, 1987.58.1, (page 48)

Horace Pippin, American, 1888 – 1946, ***Interior***, 1944, oil on canvas, 61.2 × 76.6 × .2 cm (24⅛ × 30⅛ × ¾ in.), National Gallery of Art, Washington, Gift of Mr. and Mrs. Meyer P. Potamkin, in Honor of the 50th Anniversary of the National Gallery of Art, 1991.42.1, (page 49)

Mark Rothko, American, 1903 – 1970, ***Hierarchical Birds***, 1944, oil on canvas, 100.7 × 80.5 cm (39⅝ × 31⅝ in.), National Gallery of Art, Washington, Gift of The Mark Rothko Foundation, Inc. 1986.43.20, © 1998 Kate Rothko Prizel & Christopher Rothko / Artists Rights Society (ARS), New York, (page 49)

Jackson Pollock, American, 1912 – 1956, ***Number 1, 1950 (Lavender Mist)***, 1950, oil, enamel and aluminum on canvas, 221 × 299.7 cm (87 × 118 in.), National Gallery of Art, Washington, Ailsa Mellon Bruce Fund, 1976.37.1, © 2011 The Pollock-Krasner Foundation / Artists Rights Society (ARS), New York (page 50)

Wayne Thiebaud, American, born 1920, ***Cakes***, 1963, oil on canvas, 152.4 × 182.9 cm (60 × 72 in.), National Gallery of Art, Washington, Gift in Honor of the 50th Anniversary of the National Gallery of Art from the Collectors Committee, the 50th Anniversary Gift Committee, and The Circle, with Additional Support from the Abrams Family in Memory of Harry N. Abrams, 1991.1.1, © Wayne Thiebaud/Licensed by VAGA, New York, NY, (page 50)

Roy Lichtenstein, American, 1923 – 1997, ***Look Mickey***, 1961, oil on canvas, 121.9 × 175.3 cm (48 × 69 in.), National Gallery of Art, Washington, Dorothy and Roy Lichtenstein, Gift of the Artist, in Honor of the 50th Anniversary of the National Gallery of Art, 1990.41.1, (page 51)

Martin Puryear, American, born 1941, ***Lever No. 3***, 1989, carved and painted wood, 214.6 × 411.5 × 33 cm (84½ × 162 x 13 in.), National Gallery of Art, Washington, Gift of the Collectors Committee, 1989.71.1, (page 51)